MR. FIZBEE
and the Little Troop

MR. FIZBEE
and the
Little Troop

ARTHUR TAYLOR

HOLT, RINEHART AND WINSTON / NEW YORK

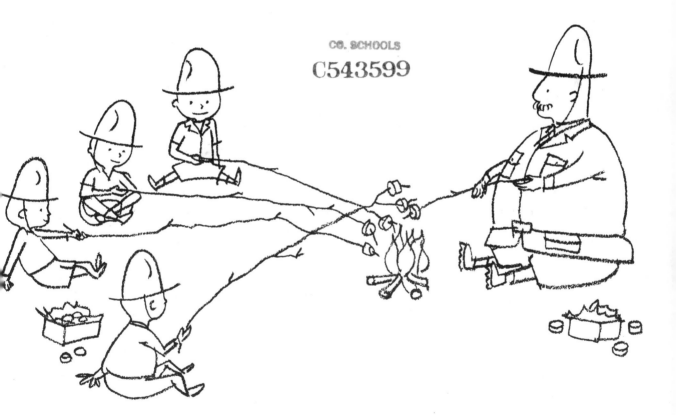

MR. FIZBEE
and the Little Troop

Mr. Fizbee lived in an
old house on Main Street
with Mrs. Fizbee, his wife.

The Fizbees had lots of little neighbors.

One day, two of the
little neighbors came up to
the big door and knocked.
"Yes?" said Mrs. Fizbee.
Well, it turned out that the
two boys wanted to see
Mr. Fizbee.
"On business," they said.

They asked him to start a
scout troop for them.
"Just for us little guys" they said.
"We're too small for the Cub Scouts,
and we want to get an early start."
Mr. Fizbee thought that
was a grand idea.

Soon he had his little troop together. They had hats and everything. One day the troop went on a hike. But because they were little scouts, they didn't go far.

Just to the back yard!

They had a fine time that day.
They hiked, ate lunch, and then
they put up the tents. Everyone
crawled into them to see
how they were.

Well, almost everyone.

And when it got dark, they camped

inside.

Oh, they had good times.
They learned to tie knots;

they played games;

and they sang songs.

They learned all about birds and animals;
they learned about signaling.

They even learned how to paddle a canoe,
and how to pay attention when
someone talks to you.

Then one day Mr. Fizbee
noticed a few empty chairs.
"Where are those boys?" he asked.
"They went to see about joining
a regular Cub Scout troop, Mr. Fizbee,"
said the smallest member. "They said
they were too big to stay in
this troop any longer."

And it was true. As time went by,
the little scouts got bigger and bigger.
They got too old for Mr. Fizbee's troop.

So, one by one, they left him.

Soon there was only one.

Then he, too, was gone.

So Mr. Fizbee went back to his gardening,

but somehow he didn't find it as much fun as it had been.

He was getting more and more tired
of gardening, when one day up ran
two small boys. "We just moved
to the neighborhood, Mr. Fizbee,"
they said. "May we join your troop?"
Mr. Fizbee began to say that he
had no troop. Then he stopped.
"Do you know anyone else who
would like to join?" he asked.

"Sure, we know lots and lots!"
the two boys said happily.
"Well, then," said Mr. Fizbee,
"go get them, and we'll have
a meeting right away."

They came from all over. More
than enough to start a new
troop. Mr. Fizbee lost no time
in getting organized. "If we
hurry," he said, "we may be
able to march in the big
parade on Saturday."

Now Mr. Fizbee has a troop again,
and he always will —

as long as he has

little neighbors.

About the Author

Arthur Taylor's first book
for children, MR. FIZBEE
AND THE LITTLE TROOP,
was begun in 1958 while he
was working toward a B.A.
degree at the Philadelphia
Museum College of Art.
After serving in the army,
he joined the N.W. Ayer
advertising agency in
Philadelphia, where he
is now an Art Director.
Mr. Taylor and his wife
live in New Jersey, and
spend the summer on
Cape May, where he paints
and photographs the
wind-swept coast.